Go for It!

Angela studied her tray. There was the mushburger, the cherry pie, the sour cream and onion potato chips, the brownie, and the banana. Angela had eaten her way through elementary school. She knew she was capable of eating everything on her tray and everything on everybody else's.

Suddenly, Angela pushed her tray away. She had made a decision.

''Yes, you can help,'' she told her friends. ''You can eat my lunch for me. I'm going on a diet.''

''No kidding?'' said Terri. ''This I've gotta see.''

But Sonya cried out: ''Go for it!''

Books by Susan Smith

Samantha Slade #1 MONSTER-SITTER
Samantha Slade #2 CONFESSIONS OF A TEENAGE FROG
Samantha Slade #3 OUR FRIEND: PUBLIC NUISANCE #1
Samantha Slade #4 THE TERRORS OF ROCK AND ROLL

Available from ARCHWAY Paperbacks

Best Friends #1 SONYA BEGONIA AND THE ELEVENTH
BIRTHDAY BLUES
Best Friends #2 ANGELA AND THE KING-SIZE CRUSADE

Available from MINSTREL Books

Best Friends™

#2 Angela and the King-size Crusade

by
Susan Smith

A MINSTREL® BOOK

PUBLISHED BY POCKET BOOKS

New York   London   Toronto   Sydney   Tokyo

A MINSTREL PAPERBACK *ORIGINAL*

 A Minstrel Book published by
POCKET BOOKS, a division of Simon & Schuster, Inc.,
1230 Avenue of the Americas, New York, N.Y. 10020

ISBN: 0-671-64041-0

First Minstrel Books printing May, 1988

10 9 8 7 6 5 4 3 2 1

A MINSTREL BOOK and colophon are registered trademarks
of Simon & Schuster, Inc.

BEST FRIENDS is a trademark of Susan Smith.

Printed in the U.S.A.

For
Jennifer Berini

Chapter One

CAN YOU ACT? CAN YOU DANCE? CAN YOU SING? IF YOU CAN DO ANY OF THE ABOVE, STAY TUNED FOR THE AUDITIONS FOR *WEST SIDE STORY*. SIGN UP NOW!!!

The notice on the bulletin board spoke to Angela King. She had decided already that she wanted to be an actress. It wouldn't be very hard because she knew she was a natural. For one thing, she was the greatest charades player she had ever met. Everybody said so.

Angela dug in her backpack for a pen and wrote her name on the sign-up sheet in her best handwriting. Then she closed her eyes and thought about herself as an actress, the audience clapping. Absentmindedly, she stepped backward, preparing to take a bow.

"Hey, Fatso, watch out!"

Angela turned around in surprise to see who was talking

to whom. A small boy who looked like a third-grader grinned up at her.

"I'm talking to you," he said, as if Angela had asked him.

"Oh, yeah?" Angela put her hands on her big hips. "You've got the wrong person, kid. My name's not Fatso."

"Coulda fooled me," the boy replied, and walked off.

He almost ruined it, Angela thought. He came along and almost wrecked the daydream, just when she was getting really into it.

She sighed, but then she caught her reflection in the glass cabinet where Gladstone Elementary's sports trophies were kept. Her face was round but okay, she decided. Her shoulder-length dark brown hair and turned-up nose were okay, too, and so were her chocolatey brown eyes. (Angela usually thought of colors in terms of food.) When she piled her hair up on top of her head, she looked older, almost fifteen, she figured.

I know I can act, she said to herself. I'll be Maria, the star of the play.

The idea grew as Angela walked outside and across the yard to the cafeteria. She got a tray and lined up with everyone else. As usual, she planned to save places for her friends who hadn't arrived yet.

Scanning the selection of food, Angela finally picked out a mushburger. (That's what she called the cafeteria burgers, because they were always mushed as though someone had sat on them.) The menu for the day also included a slice of cherry pie or a dish of Jell-O, a bag of potato chips, and a carton of chocolate milk. Angela piled her tray high—with the menu items and more. As she turned toward the tables, she collided with someone else.

"Hey, klutz, look where you're going!" an indignant voice cried.

The voice belonged to Celia Forester, the red-haired beauty and snobbiest sixth-grader of Gladstone Elementary. Celia glared at Angela, holding her tray tightly as her food ran together.

"Geez, you almost knocked me over," Celia complained, tossing her head back. "It's like running into a horse."

"My feelings exactly," Angela retorted.

Celia didn't seem to hear her. Instead, she stared at Angela's tray. "Wow, do you really eat all that food? Boy, a hamburger, cherry pie, potato chips, a brownie, and a banana. You've practically got two lunches there. No wonder."

"No wonder what?" Angela replied, but as soon as the words were out of her mouth, she regretted them.

"Ha! Well, if you don't know, *I'm* not going to tell you," Celia said. She slithered by Angela, her nose in the air.

"Watch your mouth, Celia," said Terri Rivera, appearing next to Angela with her own tray. Then Angela's other friends, Dawn Selby and Sonya Plummer, joined them. All of a sudden Angela felt a lot better. It was easier to face Celia with her friends around.

"Yeah, watch your mouth," Angela repeated, feeling satisfied. She knew that Celia was unhappy at home, but that wasn't any excuse for her to insult Angela. And it was hard to remember to feel sorry for Celia when Celia was being so mean.

Celia shot her a disgusted glance, but didn't say anything else.

"We should hang her by her thumbs," Sonya said loyally, plunking her tray down on the table where the four friends usually sat.

Angela grinned. Just a few weeks earlier, Sonya, who had moved back to Gladstone after a year in New York City, had been friends with Celia Forester. But that hadn't lasted long. Celia had turned out to be a traitor—which had shown Sonya who her true friends were. Now she and Angela and Dawn and Terri were even going to start a private group called the High Visibility Club, to make them more noticeable around school.

Angela sat down on the bench between Sonya and Terri. Her friends automatically moved aside to make more room for her, since Angela's thighs seemed to ooze over the seat.

"I want to be in the school play," Angela announced. "Do you know what we're putting on this year?"

Her friends shook their heads.

"West Side Story," Angela informed them. "I saw the notice for auditions."

"What part do you want?" Sonya asked.

"I want to be Maria, the star," declared Angela.

Everyone was silent.

"We have the same color hair," she went on.

"You'd be the perfect Maria," agreed Terri. "Except that you're twice her size."

"Terri," said Dawn warningly.

Angela frowned. "Yeah, thanks a lot," she said. "Some friend you are. And I bet you don't believe I can do it. But I can. I can be a great actress."

"Ignore The Mouth," Dawn offered, her blond bangs hanging over her blue eyes. "She doesn't mean what she says. Besides, there are fat actresses."

"I don't want to be a *fat* actress. I don't want to be a fat anything!" Angela cried. "I just want the best part in the play, and I'm going to get it."

"Wow. This *is* serious," said Sonya.

Angela sighed. "I can't stand it anymore," she said, unwrapping her mushburger. "I think I have to lose weight."

The others stared at her, then at her tray.

"What's the matter with you guys?" Angela demanded. She took a big bite of the burger.

"Oh, nothing, Angie," Sonya said quickly. "I just wonder how you're going to be able to do that. It's not easy, you know."

"Yeah. You do eat sort of, well, a lot," Dawn added.

"Enough for ten people," Terri couldn't resist saying.

Angela stopped mid-bite. "So what? I can eat less," she said defensively.

"Really?" Terri raised her thick, dark eyebrows.

"Sure. I just never tried it before." Angela put her mushburger back on her tray. "It shouldn't be too hard."

The others nodded and started to open their sandwiches.

"Anyway, remember—we started the High Visibility Club to do things that will make people notice us," she went on.

"You'd have a hard time being invisible," Terri said, and snickered. The others ignored her.

"You've got a point, Angie," Sonya said.

"Maybe we could help," suggested Dawn. "What can we do?"

Angela studied her tray. The things on it were not exactly diet food. At least Angela didn't think they were. She wasn't sure because she always ate whatever she felt like eating, and didn't give a thought to dieting. There was the mushburger, the cherry pie, the sour cream and onion potato chips, the brownie, and the banana. Angela had eaten her way through elementary school. She knew she was capable of eating everything on her tray and everything on everybody else's.

Suddenly, Angela pushed her tray away. She had made a decision.

"Yes, you can help," she told her friends. "You can eat my lunch for me. I'm going on a diet."

Sonya and Dawn and Terri looked at Angela as if she'd gone bonkers. Dawn gasped in surprise. Sonya dropped her spoon, splattering yogurt on her T-shirt. And Terri whistled softly.

"No kidding?" she said. "This I've gotta see."

But Sonya cried out: "Go for it!"

Chapter Two

☘

Angela made straight for the refrigerator when she got home.

"There's a delectable Key Lime pie in there, Angie," her mother called from the living room.

"Thanks, Mom," Angela replied. But she had no intention of touching the Key Lime pie.

Dawn, Terri, and Sonya were with her, and Angela was determined to stick to her diet. She handed out soda, cookies, and chips to her friends, but took only a glass of water for herself.

"Hurry up," said Dawn. "The show's about to begin."

"Okay," said Angela. She led the way into the den and turned on the big color TV. Every Wednesday afternoon the four friends gathered to watch "Maureen Montclair," a series about a girl detective.

"Maureen is so thin," cried Angela during the first commercial. She hadn't noticed that before.

"She's got a great personality, too," Dawn pointed out.

"Angela's got a great personality," said Sonya. "She's Miss Personality."

"Yeah, she could make friends with an ax murderer," Terri said, laughing.

"I hope not!" Dawn exclaimed.

Angela giggled. "Thanks. Big on personality—and size."

"King-size," Terri quipped. "Just like your name."

Angela groaned. "Cute, Terri. Why couldn't my last name be Thin?"

"Angela Thin?" giggled Dawn.

An advertisement for potato chips came on, and Dawn pointed at the plump actress who was popping a giant chip in her mouth.

"Now look. There's a—a, um, heavy actress," she said.

"Exactly. Do you realize what that ad *really* says?" Angela cried. She mimicked the narrator's enthusiastic voice. "You too can be fat and jolly by eating these potato chips." She flopped back on the couch. "I never want to be like that. I hope you guys notice that the people who get the best parts are skinny."

"Like Maureen," agreed Sonya, as the show came back on. "She looks great in that outfit."

Angela looked at Maureen's peppermint pink jumpsuit.

It was an outfit designed for skinny people—not for some-one of her size.

"I think you should get into exercise," said Terri sud-denly, sounding helpful for once. "Maybe you could take gymnastics with me."

"I used to take dancing lessons with Sonya," Angela reminded her, but she hadn't really enjoyed them.

"You could get up early and do exercises with Jack La Lanne," suggested Dawn. "My mom does that every morning before work."

"You can come over and use my gym equipment any time, Angie," Terri went on. "I bet you'll get skinny fast."

"Thanks, Terri!" said Angela.

"I'll cut out recipes for you," said Sonya. "My mom gets all these magazines. You'll probably have to eat a lot of cottage cheese."

"I like cottage cheese."

"Then it's all settled," declared Terri, who liked to have things solved quickly.

"What's all settled, girls?" Angela's mother sailed into the room. She was wearing one of her familiar Hawaiian print dresses. It flowed over her huge body like a curtain.

Angela had never realized how big her mother was. Everyone seemed to have to move over in order to make room for her. "What're you watching? 'Maureen' again?" asked Mrs. King. "Angie, we're trying Carmine's to-night," she went on. "It's new and I've heard rave re-views, so I've got to find out for myself."

Angela looked at her friends. They shook their heads. This wasn't something they'd counted on.

"Uh, Mom," Angela began, but her mother wasn't listening.

"I made reservations for two. It's very casual so wear whatever you like." Mrs. King scooped up a handful of potato chips. "I'm surprised you didn't touch the pie. It's fantastic. So delicate. The pastry is out of this world. The recipe came in on Monday. I just had to test it." She laughed gaily.

Ellen King was a critic and writer for *Food Sense* Magazine, which meant that she spent a lot of time in restaurants. She and Angela had sampled the best and worst restaurants in town. Ellen was also a fabulous cook, and could never wait to try a new recipe.

Angela was a friend as well as a daughter to her mom. She thought her mother was exciting, funny, and smart. They ate out together three or four times a week. And Ellen King talked a lot about food—in a way no one else did. You couldn't *not* eat something great after she described it.

Angela realized that telling her mom about the diet would be hard.

"Well, I'm just going to change into my 'critic's' clothes," said Angela's mother laughingly. It amused her that she had to be "unknown" so no one would guess who she was. The magazine didn't want restaurants fixing anything special for their critic in order to get a good review.

It was better if the chef was surprised. So Angela's mom chose dark and unnoticeable clothes to wear to restaurants.

"Maureen Montclair" ended as Mrs. King left the room.

"I guess you can't really start your diet until tomorrow, Angie," said Dawn sympathetically.

"Yeah, well, I'll tell Mom about it tonight," Angela replied.

Her friends left. Angela turned off the television and then went to her room to dress for dinner.

As they drove to the restaurant later, Angela thought about Maureen Montclair and how beautiful she looked. Maureen was so slender and moved so gracefully. Her voice was soft (except when she was talking to villains) and her face was perfect.

"Remember that bird's nest soup we had at Sun Foo's downtown?" her mother was saying. "I understand it's not as good as it used to be. We'll have to go back there and check it out."

"Sure," Angela mumbled, because this was the kind of conversation they always had.

They sat at a table in the back of Carmine's. A salad dripping with Thousand Island dressing was served first. Angela took a couple of little bites. Her mother opened her mouth and inserted a lump of lettuce, chewing slowly to savor every flavor.

"Hmmm. This is good, Angie," she declared. "What do you think of yours? You've hardly touched it."

"It's great, Mom," Angela replied, and she needed every ounce of her willpower not to gobble it down.

Next came a pasta dish with sausage and mushrooms, and a serving of lasagne. Angela loved pasta.

"Oh, just look at the way the cheese stretches," Mrs. King said lovingly. "It's such healthy, fresh cheese. And there's fresh basil in the sauces. Did you notice that, Angela?"

"Yes, Mom," Angela replied dutifully. Her mouth watered. She took a bite of lasagne and stretched the cheese out as her mother did, then twirled it around her tongue. She decided to eat this dinner. It would be her last fling before her diet really began. But halfway through, long before she stuffed herself so full that she could barely stand up, she stopped eating.

"Honey, what's wrong? You're not very involved with your food," her mother said.

"I'm trying not to eat as much," Angela told her carefully.

"Whyever not?" her mother exclaimed. "Don't you like the food? Don't you think it's as good as Luigi's?"

"It's just as good as Luigi's, maybe better," Angela told her. "I like it fine. It's just that, well, Mom, I'm going to go on a diet."

Her mother frowned. "A diet? But why? You're not fat."

"People at school call me Fatso sometimes," Angela said.

"Well, they're wrong. You should realize that, dear. You're very pretty."

"Maybe, but I *am* overweight. And I want to try out for the school play. I want a skinny part," Angela explained. "If I can lose some weight, I've got a chance."

"I guess I can understand that. For the sake of art, it makes sense," Mrs. King said. "Shelley Winters had to gain weight to be in that movie about the shipwreck—I forget what it was called."

"I think it was the *Titanic,* but I'm not sure," Angela said. Actually, she thought that Shelley Winters *was* the *Titanic.*

"Oh, I know. It was *The Poseidon Adventure*—the same kind of story as the *Titanic.* So what are you going to order now when we go out?" Ellen asked.

Angela shrugged. "Napkins and salad."

"I might have to find another eating pal," Mrs. King said, smiling sadly at her daughter.

"Oh, Mom, don't worry. We'll still have fun," Angela assured her, feeling guilty.

"Sure we will, honey." Her mother patted her hand. Then she turned her attention back to the food. "The sausage is wonderful, Angela. There's just the right amount of fennel in it. I haven't made sausage in such a long time."

"Not since I was a baby," Angela remembered.

"Has it been that long?" Mrs. King shook her head in amazement. "I'll have to try it again." She speared the last of Angela's sausage with her fork. Angela was glad to see the sausage go.

Angela waited for her mom to ask for the check. Instead, Mrs. King said, "Oh, Angie, how about dessert? Shall we have the flan and cappucino?" She lowered her voice conspiratorially. "I hear they have a yummy caramel flan."

Angela rolled her eyes. She loved dessert. And using willpower was harder than she'd thought it would be. "Sure, Mom. I guess I'll start my diet tomorrow."

Chapter Three

⚘

"Angela, if you want to be a real actress, you've got to stop eating," declared Terri.

The four friends were at Terri's house for a meeting of the High Visibility Club. They had gathered in the Riveras' rec room, which was outfitted with all kinds of sports equipment. Terri was bouncing on the trampoline as she talked.

Angela sat on the stationary bicycle, watching her friends devour warm, homemade chocolate chip cookies. Her mouth watered, and it was hard to concentrate on what Terri was saying.

"If you don't stop eating, the only part you'll be good for this year is the Gladstone Gopher," Terri went on.

The Gladstone Gopher was the school mascot. Every year the students voted on a person to fill that position— and the chubby gopher costume.

"I guess I *am* big enough to win," Angela replied mournfully.

"Are there any blimps in *West Side Story?*" asked Terri. "I can't remember."

"No, dummy, there aren't any blimps in *West Side Story,*" Angela answered, mimicking Terri's tone of voice. "And I wish you'd quit making fat jokes."

"Okay, okay," said Terri.

The plate of cookies sat in front of Angela. She picked one up, counted the number of chips, and put it down again. "That does it. I'm on a diet starting now. For real. I even told my mom about dieting."

The others stared at her expectantly.

"How'd she take it?" asked Dawn.

"Pretty well," said Angela. "I'll still go out with her to restaurants, but I'll only eat appetizers and salads—without the dressing."

"Hey, good for you," cried Sonya.

"I ate dessert last night," Angela continued. "But it won't happen again. The diet is serious now."

"Okay, you guys," Terri began, swinging her long legs off the side of the trampoline, "let's get to work. Let's start this meeting."

The girls huddled close together while Terri kept talking. "We have to decide whether we want to have officers, or take notes, or collect money with this club," she said.

"I don't think we need officers," said Sonya. "We're in this as equals."

"And we don't have enough money to give to the club," put in Dawn. "Besides, remember we collected dues when we had our other club and we ran into a little problem with somebody spending all the money?"

"Right." Everyone shot meaningful looks at Terri, who turned bright red. Two years ago the girls had formed the DATS Club. (DATS stood for Dawn, Angela, Terri, and Sonya.) Terri was the one who had borrowed money from the club treasury so that they could buy an exercise machine.

Terri cleared her throat. "Each of us should decide how we want to be visible and then we can help each other reach our goals."

"That's a great idea!" cried Dawn, who was enthusiastic about nearly everything.

Terri handed Dawn a sheet of notebook paper. "Okay, you write down our goals. We want to be highly visible, but we don't want to be just *any* kind of visible."

"Right. For instance, a person who throws up in the middle of assembly is highly visible. But nobody wants to be her," suggested Dawn.

Terri gave her a fierce look. "Uh, right, Dawn," she said. "Can anybody think of anything else we don't want to be?"

"We don't want to be fat," Angela announced seriously. "We don't want to be the fattest girls in school, or the ugliest. We want to be the most beautiful and most accomplished."

"And better than Celia Forester," added Sonya.

"That's right," said Dawn, then bit her lip. "Hey, do you think being lunch monitor for the month counts as accomplished?" Dawn's month as lunch monitor had just begun, and she hoped it would count as *some*thing.

"That isn't exactly glamorous," Sonya pointed out.

"It's an important job, though," said Angela. "Someone has to do it."

"Yeah. Just think what the cafeteria would be like without one. We could get food poisoning," said Terri, giggling.

"Or we could get a lot of spaghetti in our hair," Dawn pointed out, beginning to giggle, too.

"I've got a super idea," said Sonya. "Let's start with Angela since she wants to lose weight. We can all help her. She'll be our first high visibility project."

"Good idea. A King-size crusade," said Terri, turning to Angela. "You can come over here after school and work out on my equipment."

"My mom has some exercise records you can listen to," said Dawn.

"We'll go to the mall on Saturday and we won't eat anything," Sonya offered.

"Thanks, guys," Angela said. What great friends she had! Usually they pigged out on pizza when they went to the mall. Things were really changing. If only Terri would keep her mouth shut sometimes.

''Meanwhile, everybody else can think of how they want to be great and visible,'' Terri added.

No one answered her. Sonya was trying to stand on her head on the trampoline. Dawn was trying to suck chocolate chips up a straw.

Terri tapped her pen on the edge of her bicycle and announced, ''This meeting is adjourned on account of extreme silliness.''

On Saturday, the four friends went to the mall. Angela brought her five-dollar allowance, which she usually spent on food. This time she used it to pay for *The Eat Anything You Want Diet Book*.

Terri didn't approve of it at all. ''If it doesn't make you suffer, Angie, how's it going to work?''

Terri was into suffering. She figured hours of pain were the only way to get anywhere in life.

''It says here that you can eat what you want, only you can't have very much of the fattening stuff and you can only have it at certain times,'' Angela explained.

''Oh, so you can eat what you want on Saturday, but then you can't eat again until one o'clock on Tuesday,'' said Terri, laughing.

''Or even Wednesday,'' Angela agreed with a grin.

The girls went into a clothing shop because Dawn had money to buy a pair of jeans. Angela looked at a rack of blouses while Dawn tried on nineteen pairs of jeans.

"I think your size is over here, Angela," Sonya called to her, pointing in the direction of the larger tops.

"I don't want to look there," Angela said. "I want to look at what I'll be able to wear when I'm skinny."

Finally, Dawn settled on a pair of jeans with rabbits embroidered on the back pockets.

When she had paid for them, Angela turned to Sonya with a sigh. "I thought we'd never get out of there," she said.

"If you had your way, we'd never go shopping at all," Sonya replied. "Your idea of shopping is running from one end of a store to the other as fast as you can."

"Yeah," Dawn chimed in. "Trying to break a world's record."

"Well, come on," said Terri, looking bored. "Let's get something to eat."

"I thought we weren't going to eat," Angela cried.

"Oh, right. I forgot. It's such a habit." Terri threw up her hands. "What're we going to do, then?"

Everyone looked at Angela.

"What's everybody looking at me for?" she exclaimed. "If you want to eat, eat. I'll have a diet soda."

"Are you sure, Angie?" Dawn asked.

"Sure, I'm sure." Angela stuffed her hands in her pockets and followed her friends. She watched them order slices of pizza, but when she got to the counter, she ordered only a diet soda.

The lady at the cash register raised one hairy eyebrow

at her, then rang up the purchase. Eighty cents. It was the smallest amount of food Angela had ever bought at the mall on a Saturday.

Angela sipped her soda and watched her friends eat. Dawn had ordered a slice of pepperoni pizza, but spent most of her time picking the pieces of pepperoni off the cheese and leaving them in a little pile on a napkin.

Sonya ate hers neatly. She took small bites and wiped her mouth after each one.

Terri was a pig. She took giant bites and let grease dribble down her chin. Angela had never noticed how gross she looked. But then she'd always concentrated on her own food, so she'd never noticed much of anything during a meal.

Angela's stomach started to growl. She opened up her diet book and looked up pizza. "A slice of plain cheese pizza contains 425 calories," the book informed her.

"Angie, how's your diet soda?" asked Sonya.

"Fine, except I don't like diet soda," she replied.

"It's worth it, though," Terri reminded her between bites, and Angela tried to agree. But it was hard with pizza staring her in the face.

At last the others began to fold up their empty paper plates and get ready to leave. A pile of pepperoni still sat on Dawn's napkin. Usually, Angela ate all the leftovers. She was proud of herself for not even reaching toward the abandoned pepperoni. Everybody noticed Angela notice the leftovers and not eat them.

"You're doing great, Angela," said Sonya. "I'm really proud of you."

"You're going to be skinny in no time," exclaimed Dawn.

"I feel skinnier already," Angela said, tossing her empty soda can into the garbage. The soda had a funny aftertaste, but she supposed she could get used to it. She supposed she could get used to almost anything.

Chapter Four

⌘

"All right, students. Please come to order," said Ms. Bell. "We have just a short time for this meeting."

About thirty students had gathered for a meeting about the auditions for *West Side Story*. Angela looked around the room to see who else was planning to try out. Of course, Celia Forester was there. She thought that just because her sister was an actress on TV, she should be an actress, too. Celia was her biggest competition, Angela decided. After all, she was skinny and pretty. But Celia had red hair, not dark brown, like Maria was supposed to have. That was important. Angela felt hopeful.

Ms. Bell handed out copies of the script to the students. Tommy Atwood, the cutest boy in the fifth grade, took a copy. Howard Tartar, the funniest boy in the fifth grade, took one, too, and passed the rest back to Angela.

"Who do you want to be?" Angela asked him.

24

Howard stuck his skinny chest out and said proudly, "Tony. Don't you think I'd make a good one?"

Angela laughed. Howard was cute, but he was short. She didn't really think he'd make a good Tony. Not like the one in the movie, anyway. The Tony in the movie was at least as tall as Maria. Howard was shorter than all the girls in the sixth grade, except Dawn.

But Angela didn't want to hurt his feelings, so she said, yes, she thought he'd make a good Tony.

"I'm romantic, too," Howard added, making a funny face.

Howard was the kind of person who was funny without even having to try. He did great animal imitations. But he always looked serious, even when he was being silly.

"Howard, would you please pay attention?" Ms. Bell called to him.

He swiveled around in his seat. "Yes, Ms. Bell," he replied sweetly. (He also did a great Ms. Bell imitation.) He sat up straight, sticking his chest out in an exaggerated way.

"And please save your acting ability for the stage," she added curtly.

The class giggled. Ms. Bell had never quite forgiven Howard for bringing wooden statues of naked people to school after his trip to Africa.

Then Angela saw Sonya in the back of the room. Oh, no, she thought. Was Sonya really planning to try out?

Angela wanted to catch Sonya after the meeting, but

Sonya left the room quickly, and Celia Forester and Jeannie Sandlin stood blocking the doorway.

"What part are you trying out for, Angela?" Celia asked, snagging her as she tried to squeeze by them.

"Maria," Angela replied.

"Maria? Really?" said Celia. She struggled to hold back a smile, but finally burst out laughing.

Tears sprang to Angela's eyes. She marched away from the girls, then broke into a run. Celia laughed like a TV actress. A villain actress.

I'll show her, Angela thought angrily.

These days, Dawn always reached the lunchroom before anyone else did, because it was her responsibility to make sure the students behaved themselves and didn't throw food around or mess up the neat stacks of trays. Most of the time, she stood guard over the garbage cans.

A bunch of second-graders dumped their food in the garbage so that it splashed all over her. "Hey, watch it, will you?" Dawn cried. "You're making a big mess."

"You're not my mother. You can't tell me what to do," one kid told her.

"Yeah, that's right," the others chimed in.

Angela came to Dawn's rescue. "Cool it, or I'll sit on you," she threatened the kids. They frowned at her, but went away. "I won't be able to do that when I'm skinny," Angela remarked. "Where's Sonya?"

"Getting lunch."

Angela walked over to the lunch line and stood with Terri and Sonya.

"Are you trying out for the play?" she asked Sonya.

Sonya looked embarrassed. "I'm thinking about it. I mean, after everything we said about being visible, I think I should."

"What about me?" demanded Angela.

"You're not the only person in the world who wants to be an actress."

"Maybe it would be better if we all auditioned. Then everyone would notice the four of us," Terri suggested.

Angela paid for her carton of strawberry yogurt. It was all she planned to eat for lunch. "I don't think that's a good idea," she argued. "If we're all doing the same thing, then everybody's going to think we're the same."

"How could they think that?" Sonya asked. "We don't *look* alike."

Angela rolled her eyes. "But if you try out, Sonya, I won't stand a chance."

"Angie, I'm not trying out for the part of Maria. I'll be . . . somebody else." But neither Sonya nor Angela could remember any other characters in the play.

"It's got a cast of thousands," said Terri, and everyone laughed. "Anyway, *I* don't want to be in it."

"Maybe I'll try out for stage manager," said Dawn, sitting down next to Angela. "I do such a great job in the cafeteria."

"No one will throw food around with you there," said Sonya. "That's for sure."

The girls started giggling again. Then they turned their attention to the play.

"Howard wants to be Tony," Angela told them.

"He's too short," Terri said.

"You can't change some things," Angela said to her friends, and they agreed.

After school the girls had a meeting at Angela's house. Usually, everyone liked having meetings there because Angela provided good snacks. This time, she served diet sodas, and carrot and celery sticks.

The four friends draped themselves over the wicker furniture in Angela's room.

Sonya yanked a shirt out of a bag and handed it to Angela. "Here. This is for you," she said. "It's too big for me, but it's too small for you now. You can shrink into it. Maybe that'll make you try harder to lose weight."

Angela held the shirt up to her chest. It was purple with yellow stripes, not exactly her style. It wasn't Sonya's style, either.

"I'll have to lose a ton before I can wear this," she said. "But thanks."

"You're welcome."

Dawn had brought along one of her mother's exercise tapes. All four of the girls tried the exercises. They were done to popular rock songs, with a woman shouting out directions.

"Push, pull, that's right! There you go, you're cooking now!" the instructor exclaimed. "Swivel those hips, to the right, to the left! And bend your knees!"

Angela panted and huffed and swiveled and bent her knees. Terri did the exercises like an expert because she worked out every day. Dawn got her hip stuck in one direction and kept moving it back and forth mechanically. Sonya was very graceful—probably the result of lots of dance lessons. She spun around with arms outstretched and smacked Angela in the mouth.

"Hey, watch out!" Angela yelped.

"Sorry, I didn't see you," Sonya said.

"Nobody doesn't see Angela," Terri replied.

Angela bristled. "Cut that out, Terri!" Then she rubbed her mouth. "You gave me a fat lip, Sonya."

"You already had one," Sonya blurted out. "Oh, I'm sorry. I didn't mean that."

"Yes, you did," Angela said.

"I did not."

"Did, too."

"Did not."

"Will you guys shut up?" Terri yelled. "You're being immature."

"Look who's talking," said Angela.

"Okay, okay. Let's do something else. Homework, for instance." Terri took control of the situation and the girls settled down with their homework. When they were finished, they went home.

After they were gone, Angela remembered a dance recital that she and Sonya had been in when they were nine years old. They had played the parts of fairies, dressed in frilly pink and white tutus. Under the hot lights with all those parents watching, Angela became nervous. She forgot her steps and collapsed in tears in the middle of the stage. So Sonya simply took her place. She just moved right in and made the show go on. She was the star, and people talked about her for days afterward.

That was a long time ago, and now they were much more mature. The same thing wasn't going to happen again. Was it?

Angela stepped on the scale and watched the needle climb upward and stop. She'd lost two pounds. The diet was working! She was really and truly losing weight!

Chapter Five

When Angela got home from school the next day, she found her mother in the kitchen making sausages.

The entire house smelled of meat and spices.

"Go ahead, Angie, taste one," her mother urged her.

"I can't eat them, Mom. Remember?" Angela wailed.

"You can eat just one."

"I'm not supposed to. My diet book says I can't eat sausages unless I don't eat for the whole day before," she insisted.

"That diet book!" Mrs. King exclaimed, moving around the kitchen like a big ship. "I'm worried about you, honey. You're not eating, and you're not having any fun."

"Who says?" Angela said. "Maybe you don't think I'm having any fun, but I'm having fun, see?" She grinned and stood on one foot.

"Well, I don't know. I made that German chocolate cake

and it's still in the refrigerator. People can't live on celery sticks alone,'' her mother went on.

"I eat lots of other things. I just don't eat as much of them as I used to, Mom," said Angela. "Besides, I'm losing weight. See? My pants are loose." Angela pulled out the waistband of her jeans to show her mother.

"Hmm. This means you'll need new clothes," Mrs. King said thoughtfully. Then she changed the subject. "We're having Indian food tonight, but I have to finish these sausages before we leave."

Angela left her mother to the sausages and went upstairs. She stepped on the scale and saw that she'd lost another half a pound. Losing weight was exciting, she thought, as she got ready to go out to dinner.

At the restaurant that night, Angela ordered salad with nothing on it.

"Angie, I was hoping you'd try one of the vegetable dishes," Mrs. King said. "You know, I like you to sample something each time we go out. Can't you at least order a dressing for the salad?"

"Okay. But I want it on the side," Angela replied.

Her mother ordered three kinds of bread and two dishes, all of which she finished. Then she finished Angela's salad after pouring the dressing over it. Angela took a couple of bites of a vegetable dish, because according to her book, she could eat small amounts of most things.

"Oh, Angela," said Mrs. King happily. "This dinner is wonderful. The bread is so light. You're really missing something. And the meat—that spicy dish was real fire. We'll have to come here again—when you're not dieting, that is.''

"I'm going to be on a diet forever," Angela declared. "I never want to be fat again."

"Darling, how many times have I told you, you're not fat," Mrs. King insisted. But Angela couldn't help noticing that as her mother lifted her water glass, her arm jiggled.

Angela sighed.

"We must have one of the desserts. I understand they're wonderful here," Mrs. King went on.

"Mom, did you ever go on a diet?" Angela asked suddenly.

"Oh, dozens of times, but I never stick to diets. Your father always wanted me to be thin. He said he was worried about my health. But I think he just wanted a slender wife."

"Really?" Angela was interested. Her mother hardly ever talked about her father. He hadn't been around since Angela was a baby. Would my father like me better if I were thin? Angela wondered. "Does my dad know what I look like?" she asked her mother.

"I don't know. Not really. I sent him a picture of you when you were eight," Mrs. King replied. "You were adorable."

"I was fat," Angela said matter-of-factly.

"Not fat. Pleasantly plump. . . . Ah, here's our dessert."

Two dishes of mango ice cream were placed on the table. One in front of Mrs. King, the other in front of Angela.

Automatically, Angela picked up her spoon, then realized what she was doing. "Mom, I didn't want this! Why'd you order it?"

"I thought you needed it, Angie. It won't hurt, and it's so good."

"I won't eat it," Angela announced, even though it looked wonderful. She felt like a two-year-old.

Her mother looked surprised. Then she smiled. "Oh, well. Okay, twist my arm. I'll eat it!"

"But you're eating twice as much dessert," Angela said.

"Doesn't matter. I have a cast-iron stomach."

When they got home that night, Angela started reading the script for *West Side Story*. It was about a girl and a boy, Maria and Tony, who belong to enemy street gangs in New York City. Tony belongs to the Jets, and Maria is part of the Sharks, although she's not an actual fighting member. They meet at a dance and fall in love at a time when the gangs are planning to have a big fight. So Tony decides that instead the gangs should stop fighting and make peace. In the end, Maria's brother, Bernardo, the leader of the Sharks, is accidentally killed by Tony, who's trying to protect Riff, the leader of the Jets. Then Tony in turn is killed.

Angela imagined that she was beautiful Maria, and that Tony loved her. But every time she thought about Tony, she pictured Howard Tartar, and laughed. Of course, Howard could be a good, short Tony, but he would be so silly. He'd make everyone laugh, even during the serious parts.

Angela stood in front of the mirror and recited some of Maria's lines. Even though she hadn't been chosen as Maria yet, Angela thought it would be helpful to pretend she was Maria—to feel the way she would feel, to do and say what she would do and say. Then she sang the song "I Feel Pretty": "I feel pretty, oh, so pretty . . ."

Her voice sounded pretty good. Angela had never thought much about singing. She eyed herself critically in the mirror. She was thinner, but she was still a plump Maria. Her hair was just right, though. It was long and dark, and she could make it fan across her shoulders. And her facial expressions were great. She was sure she was a better choice for Maria than either Sonya or Celia was.

Then Angela thought about writing to her father and telling him she was going to play Maria. He would probably be impressed and tell all his friends. Then he would also guess that she was not a fat person.

Angela put on the tape Dawn had given her and did her exercises faithfully. Her muscles didn't hurt as much now. Her fat didn't jiggle the way it used to. That's because there wasn't as much fat. She saw definite improvements.

Angela turned on her TV. She watched an advertisement for cake mixes, and one for TV dinners. Then a documentary came on. It was called "The Battle of the Bulge" and was about people who have their stomachs stapled up so that they can't eat as much. And because they can't eat as much, of course, they lose weight. They showed "before" and "after" pictures of the people who had had the stapling done. Most of them looked great.

However, they showed the operation, which was gross. Angela decided she couldn't go through with it. Stomach stapling was awful.

Angela had to look away from the TV screen, and when she did, she noticed a picture on her dresser that her mom had taken of her a couple of months earlier at a friend's swimming pool. Angela looked blimpy. The photo gave her an idea. She cut out a piece of white paper and stuck it to the bottom of the picture. Then she wrote "BEFORE" under it in red puffy letters. She thumbtacked the picture to the corner of her mirror.

Now she could look forward to the "AFTER" picture. When she got the "AFTER" picture, she knew exactly what she would do. She would send the picture away to have it blown up to poster size.

The documentary ended and an ad for chocolate came on. The chocolate was poured from a big metal container and rippled over a candy bar. Angela's mouth watered. How could they make a stomach-stapling documentary and then show all these yummy food ads? How did anybody ever lose weight?

Dieting wasn't easy. The world was full of forbidden food.

Angela was glad she was such a strong person.

Chapter Six

8

Angela was hungry, and food was everywhere. Her house was full of food, her friends' houses were full of food, and there was nowhere that food didn't show up.

The owner of a restaurant that Mrs. King had given a good review sent her some free tickets to an amusement park.

"If you and your friends would like to go, I'll take you to the park on Saturday," Mrs. King told Angela. "I'm having lunch with Sam that day. He's going to tell me about a job I might apply for."

"Really?" Angela was interested.

"Don't say anything to anyone," her mother warned her. "I don't want the people at *Food Sense* to know I'm looking."

"I won't. Don't worry," she said.

Angela perked up at the mention of Sam. Secretly, she

wished her mother would marry Sam, even though Sam wasn't very romantic. He was skinny as a rail and looked sort of weird next to Mrs. King, but he was nice. Every once in a while he came over for dinner, and he brought Angela things like smoked salmon and tortilla chips. Angela hoped he could break the habit.

On Sunday, the girls did their exercises at Terri's, then went over to Angela's so Mrs. King could drive them to the amusement park. When she dropped them off, she promised to pick them up at five o'clock.

At first, the girls just walked around, looking at everything. Then they decided to go in the Fun House, a house full of wobbly-looking mirrors, big slides, slanted floors, and even a maze.

Angela, wearing a green shirt, stepped in front of a mirror that made her look like a giant stepped-on watermelon. She screeched. Then she stood in front of one that made her look like a green bean, with an unnaturally long head and feet. All the girls giggled.

"I wish I had this mirror at home," said Angela. "Then I'd always look thin."

"No, you'd always look like a pinhead," said Sonya.

The girls went down the slide three times each. The last time, they landed in a heap on top of each other.

Terri disentangled herself from her friends. "I'm starved," she exclaimed. "Let's go find something to eat."

"Great idea," everyone agreed. Everyone except Angela, that is, even though her stomach was growling.

"What'll we have?" Dawn asked. "They've got everything here."

"Everything but diet food," Angela replied. All she could see were displays of cotton candy, candy apples, hot dogs, and French fries.

Terri led the way to a food stand. She and Dawn and Sonya spent a long time looking over the selection.

"A diet soda, please," Angela said, feeling impatient.

"Gee, Angie, you look thinner just since yesterday," observed Sonya. "Why don't you order something?"

Angela shook her head. "I want to be even thinner. Auditions are next week, remember? And I still don't look a thing like Maria."

Sonya and Dawn and Terri finally made their selections.

Angela couldn't help but notice what they ordered. Terri ordered a cheeseburger with fries and a milkshake. Sonya ordered a hot dog with the works and a soda. And Dawn picked out a chocolate milkshake and deep-fried artichoke hearts.

Angela breathed in the odor of the artichokes. She loved artichokes in any form. But she found that she didn't love watching someone else eat them when she couldn't.

Dawn noticed Angela staring at her plate. "Are you sure you don't want some?" she asked, holding out a piece.

"I'll just have a bite, thanks," Angela answered.

"You're doing so well," said Terri. "Why don't you treat yourself just this once?"

"No, I can't treat myself," insisted Angela, taking a big swallow of her soda to wash down the artichoke. She was actually beginning to like diet soda.

"Don't you want a bite of cheeseburger?" asked Terri, sticking her cheeseburger in Angela's face.

Angela drew back. "Terri, aren't you the one who always says people have to suffer to get what they want?" Angela asked.

"Yeah, that's me," Terri said with her mouth full. "But I just can't stand to see you suffer."

"That's tough," said Angela. "I have to suffer."

"What happened to *The Eat Anything You Want* book?" asked Sonya.

"It's great, except that there's nothing here that comes in small amounts," explained Angela. "That piece of artichoke was my lunch."

"That's downright cruelty," exclaimed Terri. "You're going to starve."

"No, I won't," replied Angela. "I'm being careful. And soon I'll be thin." She sighed heavily. "Is lunch over yet?"

Her friends were still chewing.

"No, relax," said Terri.

Finally, the girls finished and made their way over to the merry-go-round and then the Ferris wheel. Dawn got sick on the Ferris wheel and started to cry.

"It was the artichokes, I know it," she blubbered. She was famous for her weak stomach.

"Let's call your mom and see if she can pick us up," Angela suggested. "My mom is off in some unknown restaurant with Sam."

Angela reached Dawn's mother, who said she'd be right there. The others went on the rides while Angela sat with Dawn and waited.

"I should never go on those awful rides," Dawn said.

"You should never go on those awful rides," Dawn's mother said when she arrived. Obviously, Dawn took after her mother. They looked like people in one of those mother-and-daughter ads. "What in the world did you eat, anyway?"

"Artichokes," Dawn said.

"Killer artichokes," Terri added.

"I thought they were great," said Angela.

With that, Dawn turned green and asked her mother to stop the car.

Chapter Seven

The auditorium echoed with the excited voices of students waiting to audition for the play. Angela stood with Sonya, Terri, and Dawn.

Celia Forester stood apart from everyone else.

"Celia acts like she's already the star," said Sonya.

"She's got plenty of competition," said Angela.

Howard approached the girls. "I've decided which part I should audition for," he announced.

Sonya and Angela looked at each other and giggled.

"I want to play Riff," said Howard. "He's the intelligent, wacky one."

"Sounds like you," Sonya told him, smiling.

Howard stuck out his chest and stood on tiptoe. "I thought so, too," he said, pleased with himself.

"I want to be Anita," said Sonya. "She's tough."

"You'd make a good one." Howard really liked Sonya.

They grinned at each other.

The drama teacher, Ms. Kerry, raised her arms to get everyone's attention.

"Now, boys and girls, as you know, there are lots of parts to be filled. Read the part of the character you'd like to play. We'll post the cast list in a couple of days." She clapped her hands again as the kids started talking. "Quiet! Celia Forester, will you go first, please?"

Terri held her nose as Celia strode proudly onto the stage, and Angela imitated Celia's walk.

Celia chose to read from the scene that took place in a bridal shop. Ms. Kerry read the part of Anita.

"One month I've been in this country. I sew all day and sit all night. Why did my brother bring me here?" asked Celia, holding out her hands dramatically. She read a few more lines before Ms. Kerry stopped her.

"Brava!" the drama teacher cried. "Next!"

Sonya was next. She auditioned with Tommy Atwood, who read the part of Bernardo, Anita's boyfriend. "You have your big important war council. Either the council or me," she sneered, her hands on her hips.

"First one and then the other." Tommy read straight from the book in a zombie voice.

Everyone giggled.

Howard went next. He chose a scene near the beginning, after a policeman, Officer Krupke, has come along to break up the gangs.

"This is our territory," Howard announced. To play

Riff, he stuck his chest out and made his voice extra deep. "We've gotta move fast and clean them up in one big fight!"

"A rumble," Tommy intoned. Everyone giggled. Tommy wasn't exactly dramatic.

Angela's turn. She had chosen a romantic scene between Maria and Tony.

She took a deep breath before walking onto the stage. Then she said, "All the world is only you and me!" and launched into song: "Tonight, tonight, It all began tonight, I saw you and the world went away . . ."

Eddie Martin took over the boy's part. "Today," he sang, "all day I had the feeling, A miracle would happen, I now know I was right."

Angela smiled and lifted her hands and sang. Then Eddie joined her as though it had all been planned. "But here you are, and what was just a world is a star . . . tonight!"

Everyone clapped—everyone except Celia, Jeannie, and their friend Polly, who wore identical frowns. Angela turned to Eddie in surprise. He was a quiet boy, a friend of Tommy Atwood's. Nobody paid much attention to him. Who knew he could sing? thought Angela.

"You were both great," Angela's friends said when she'd left the stage.

"Why didn't we know you could sing?" asked Terri.

Angela shrugged, pleased with herself. "You never asked me."

Ms. Kerry approached her.

"That was wonderful, Angela," she said. "I know we'll have a part for you."

Angela beamed. Then she heard Ms. Kerry say almost the same thing to Eddie.

And *then* she saw her mother sweep into the auditorium, grinning. Mrs. King rushed to Angela.

"Angela! You were fabulous!" she cried, embracing her.

Angela could hear people snickering. She had never been so embarrassed! When she finally pulled away, she saw that everyone was looking at her mother in her huge gray caftan. The caftan made her look like a whale.

"I just came from lunch, honey, and I stopped in to see your audition. I watched from the hallway," she said. "Your performance was delicious. It certainly outshines lunch. I really wish chefs would learn to make a chef's salad correctly."

Angela was ready to die. "Mom, we have to get back to class," she interrupted.

Ellen clapped her hand to her face. "Of course," she said. "I'll see you later." She left the auditorium, her dress rustling.

The four friends walked back to their classes together. Celia followed them.

"Like mother, like daughter, Angie," she chanted.

"Hey, who asked you, Toothpick?" Angela shot back, hurt.

"She's just jealous, Angie," said Sonya comfortingly.

"Why? Because she wants to be a blimp, too?" Angela grumbled.

"No, because you sang well and got more attention than anyone else. Celia can't stand it when she's not the big cheese."

"I wish I could crawl into a hole," moaned Angela. "My mom really embarrasses me."

"My mom embarrassed me when she married Bob Stretch," said Sonya. "He's just a goofy cowboy. Worst of all, sometimes people think he's my father."

"At least he won't take up the whole auditorium when he comes to see the play," Angela grumbled. "I wish my mom would go on a diet. But how can you ask someone like her to stop eating? The other day she actually made sausages. Can you believe that?"

"Did you eat any?" asked Terri.

"No. I have to keep reminding her I'm on a diet," Angela said. "There's always a chocolate something in the refrigerator. Cookies here, pie there."

"It's the way your mother talks that really does it," Dawn observed. "She could make cardboard sound delicious."

The girls decided Dawn was right. And Angela decided that living with a mother like hers was really going to test her willpower.

On Friday morning the results of the audition were posted in the hallway in front of the attendance office. Angela, Terri, Dawn, and Sonya peered over the crowd to try to read it. This is what they saw:

CAST

The Jets

Riff, the leader	Howard Tartar
Tony, his friend	Eddie Martin
Action	Robbie Song
Rosalia	Sonya Plummer

The Sharks

Bernardo, the leader	Tommy Atwood
Maria, his sister	Celia Forester
Anita, Bernardo's girl	Angela King
Chino, Bernardo's friend	Jack Barry

There were lots of other characters in the cast, but these were some of the most important.

Terri backed away from the announcement, glowering fiercely. "So, Celia got the lead part. It's not fair."

"Not fair at all," agreed Angela, who felt as if she had been socked in the stomach.

"But Angie, you're going to be Anita," Sonya said. "That was the part I wanted. Anita gets to do a lot of singing."

"I know," Angela replied, "but I wanted to be Maria. I really wanted to be a star." She turned her head away, trying not to cry, and saw Celia surrounded by a bunch of boys, including Tommy Atwood and Eddie Martin. She was smiling.

"Now doesn't that make you sick?" said Terri.

"I can't understand the attraction myself," said Dawn.

"She's acting like a big shot already," added Angela.

Howard stopped to read the cast list, but he didn't even smile when he saw his name. "Congratulations, everyone," he said. Then he hopped down the hall singing, "I feel pretty, and witty, and gay . . ." from one of the songs in the play.

"I'm glad somebody's happy," grumbled Angela. Tears gathered in her throat, and she turned and headed for the girls' room, so that the others wouldn't see her cry.

Chapter Eight

🎴

Angela watched her mother devour a lump of garlic bread.

"I didn't get the job, Angie," Mrs. King told her.

"I'm sorry, Mom." Angela took her mother's hand.

"They want to hire a TV food critic who will sit with her back to the camera so no one will know who she is. But you know what they said to me?"

"No."

"They said they'd hire me if I lost weight, but that I couldn't appear on TV like this. Can you imagine? With all my experience? Why does it have to be a thin world when life is full and rich?" Mrs. King said dramatically, biting into another piece of garlic bread.

"You can go on a diet with me, Mom," Angela suggested.

"How? I have to eat to survive," Mrs. King said.

"That's true."

"But maybe I could diet when I'm not working," her mother went on.

Mrs. King then began studying diet recipes and writing a series of columns on diet foods for *Food Sense*. Angela was happy. Dieting was much easier with low-calorie foods around. And the fact that her mother had lost the TV job because she was overweight made Angela even more determined to become thin.

Rehearsals for the play started the following week. Angela and Sonya rehearsed their lines together after school, while Dawn and Terri watched and made comments.

Angela discovered that Anita was a more mature character than Maria was. She was also not a fat person. I can get thin roles now, she thought happily.

One day the girls practiced at Dawn's house, which was always in turmoil, because Dawn had two brothers and two sisters who were very active and noisy.

Angela and Sonya rehearsed a song about America. In the middle, Angela suddenly stopped singing.

"What's wrong?" asked Sonya.

"Why'd you screech in my ear?" Angela demanded.

"I didn't screech, I'm singing," Sonya replied indignantly. "My character is supposed to sing like that."

"You hurt my ear."

Tammy, Dawn's six-year-old sister, stepped between them. "Look what Peter gave me," she said. (Peter was her big brother.) She pulled something from her pocket and threw it on the floor. It was plastic barf.

Angela groaned. Dawn screamed. Tammy laughed.

"It's only plastic, you guys," said Terri disgustedly. "Where'd you get it?"

"Peter bought it at the joke store," Tammy said, beaming.

"It's gross," said Sonya.

"I think that I'm going to be sick," choked Dawn. "Mo-om!"

Dawn's mother came running in and whisked Tammy out of the room, but not before Tammy called over her shoulder, "He bought sneezing powder, too."

"Back to work, guys," ordered Terri.

Angela and Sonya found that much of school rehearsals was just waiting around to practice parts. Most of the kids sat in the auditorium and did their homework or read until they were called.

Everybody except Celia. Whenever Angela was rehearsing, Celia interrupted to ask Ms. Kerry questions.

"Oh, Ms. Kerry, can you tell me what I should look like when I'm seeing Tony for the first time?" she asked one afternoon.

Angela glared at Celia. If Ms. Kerry hadn't been standing right there, she would've told Celia to go suck an egg.

Ms. Kerry replied, "Celia, we can discuss this later. I'm working with Angela now."

"But I want to practice the look," Celia insisted.

Ms. Kerry would not be swayed. "Celia, you'll just have to wait until Angela and I are finished."

Angela smiled. It was worth not being the star just to see Celia miserable when she thought she wasn't getting enough attention.

Ms. Kerry showed Angela how to use her hands while she was singing, and how to talk to make Anita come off as the strong character she was. Angela realized that she was proud to be Anita, because she was beginning to seem like a great character. Furthermore, she had to admit, Celia really was Maria-like, and Angela really was Anita-like. Ms. Kerry had made smart choices.

After another rehearsal a week later, Celia took Angela by the elbow, tipped her head slightly to one side, and said, "Angela, I didn't know you were on a diet."

Angela thought it was obvious, considering all the weight she'd lost, but all she replied was, "Who said I was?"

"Your mother's column," said Celia. "My mother saw it, and it said you were on a diet."

Angela cringed. She hardly ever read her mom's columns, so she didn't know what was in the latest one.

"Big deal," said Angela.

"Yeah, so what?" said Terri from behind her.

By now a crowd had gathered around the girls. Angela felt embarrassed. It was one thing to lose weight. It was quite another for your mother to tell the world about your diet. She looked down at the floor.

"I just thought it was so *cute* that your mom said you're eating so much lettuce," Celia went on. "You're lucky it doesn't show."

Angela gritted her teeth. Suddenly she felt like she weighed two hundred pounds.

"Isn't it funny that your mom makes her living by eating?" Celia laughed brightly.

Sonya giggled. Celia's friends began to laugh, too.

Terri elbowed her way between Angela and Celia. "Shut your face, Celia," she ordered.

"Yeah, bug off," Angela added, feeling her face grow hot.

Ms. Kerry came over at that moment. "Girls, what's this all about?"

"Oh, nothing," said Celia airily. "We're just talking about Angela's mother."

"No more arguments, please. Rehearsal's over," Ms. Kerry said, with a sigh of exasperation.

"Boy," scoffed Terri as the girls watched Celia walk away. "Celia made it sound as if it was all our fault."

"Sonya, what were *you* laughing at?" demanded Angela.

Sonya giggled all over again. "It just sounded funny. Your mom *does* eat for a living, Angie."

"But it's not funny." Angela was close to tears. "How'd you like it if she was talking about *your* mom?" she cried. She stomped away from her friends and walked home by herself. She was mad at Sonya for laughing, but she was also mad that Sonya had gotten herself in the play. Angela thought that each member of the High Visibility Club should do something different. That would make them even more visible. Even though she felt a little guilty about it, Angela wanted to be the only one of her friends who was in the play.

When Angela got home, she located the most recent copy of *Food Sense* and paged through it until she found her mother's column. It was all about dieting and eating out with Angela.

My daughter Angela encouraged me to diet. At first I thought it was terrible to go to the best restaurants in town and order lettuce. But Angela has made a study of lettuce. Her observations are crisp and ahead of their time.

"You're reading the column, Angie," Mrs. King exclaimed when she poked her head in her daughter's room.

"Why did you have to put me in it?" wailed Angela.

Then she poured out the whole story of Celia and her rude comments.

"Angela, you shouldn't let what people say upset you so much," her mother told her. "You're doing something good for yourself. Don't let anybody tell you any differently. And try not to be so sensitive. Come on, let's go out. I'm working tonight."

Working meant eating, and that night they were off to a French restaurant. Angela looked at the menu and drooled. She saw a veal dish that she absolutely loved. She hadn't eaten much all day. Would it hurt to eat what she wanted just once? Probably not, she decided, especially when, as far as Celia and her friends were concerned, Angela would be a fat person no matter how much weight she lost.

"I'm having the veal," Angela announced.

"Are you sure, honey?" her mother asked. "You can have a salad."

"I'm splurging. I've been on this diet forever. Just don't write about this in your column."

Angela ordered the veal, and her mother ordered chicken in a vermouth sauce. The veal was scrumptious—baby mushrooms and parsley surrounding a tender piece of meat. Every bite melted in Angela's mouth. She decided that she could eat five small portions for the next five days to make up for what she'd done.

"What about dessert, Angie?" asked Mrs. King. "They have this delightful little torte here."

"There's nothing little about a torte, Mom," said Angela knowingly. Tortes were layered cakes with cream fillings. But a waiter passed by with the dessert tray then, loaded with iced cakes, tortes, and berry and cream concoctions. That tray was worth thousands and thousands of calories.

Angela took a deep breath. "I'm having dessert," she

declared. If no one could tell she'd been on a diet, then what would one little dessert matter?

Mrs. King smiled. "That's right. Live a little. I want to encourage you with our diet, Angie, but you deserve some treats, too, dear."

Angela tried to think thin as the slice of cake was placed in front of her.

Chapter Nine

⚘

Angela and her friends went to the mall to buy jeans to wear in the play. The costumes were black T-shirts and black jeans for everybody except Celia, who would be dressed part of the time in a frilly white dress.

Angela was mad that Celia was allowed to wear something different, and would stand out in the cast. "I'm buying a red T-shirt instead of a black one," she announced. "I want to be visible."

"That's not fair, Angie," said Sonya.

Angela glared at her. "I can do anything I want," she said. She was still mad at Sonya for laughing at Celia's rude comment.

"Ms. Kerry's gonna be mad at you," Sonya warned her.

"I don't care," Angela replied stubbornly. "It's not fair that Celia gets to wear a dress and we all have to look the same."

"I agree. Maybe you should wear something different, too, Sonya," suggested Terri.

"*I* don't want to get in trouble," said Sonya.

"What a goody-goody," retorted Angela, and Sonya frowned at her.

They tried on jeans. Angela stared at herself in the mirror. She hadn't gained any weight since the veal meal, but she hadn't lost any since then, either. She looked the same as she had looked a week ago. The pounds had stopped coming off. When Angela squeezed herself into the tight black jeans, she could see definite bulges. She was sure that people would laugh at her.

Sonya, on the other hand, looked great in her outfit. Angela hated her for being so skinny. It wasn't fair.

"Try a bigger size," suggested Sonya.

"I don't want a bigger size," replied Angela. She decided to buy the tight jeans even though she looked like a sausage in them. But then she found a great red T-shirt to cover the bulges and everyone agreed that she looked pretty good.

The girls went over to Terri's house to rehearse and to play charades. Terri's mom had left popcorn and nachos for them to eat.

"Angela, you can eat something now," urged Sonya.

"I can't," she replied. "Hey, don't you guys care about me at all? I can't lose weight if you're always trying to stuff my face."

"You're no fun, though," complained Sonya. "You never join in."

"I'm not going to be any fun if I'm fat," she said. "Whoever said fat is fun?"

"It must've been someone famous like Shakespeare," replied Terri, laughing.

"You just don't want me to be a big success," complained Angela. "You guys are always eating."

"We always *did* eat. You just didn't notice because you were so busy eating, too," Dawn pointed out.

"That's right," said Sonya.

"Hey!" exclaimed Terri. "You're not a party pooper, Angie, you're a food pooper."

"That's not fair," said Angela. "What are you guys doing? I thought you wanted to help me. What happened to the High Visibility Club?"

"Hey, gang," said Dawn. "Let's not fight. Let's do something else. How about charades?"

Grumbling, they gave up the argument.

During charades, Angela guessed all but one of the answers, which meant she was still the champ.

Then the girls sang "I Feel Pretty." Sonya kept interrupting at the wrong times and singing so loudly that Angela couldn't hear herself. She yelled at Sonya. Terri yelled at Angela. Dawn yelled at Terri. Everyone was tired and mad.

Angela went home and did her exercises. Sometimes she wondered about her friends. Why did Sonya have to make so much noise? Did she want to be the only person who got attention in the play?

Angela sincerely hoped that the play wouldn't turn out the way the dance recital had two years earlier.

Angela exercised until she was sweaty, then tried on her jeans. They barely zipped up. She was the same size as she had been a few hours before when she'd bought them. She told herself not to be discouraged—but it was hard to listen.

Angela put her *West Side Story* cassette in the tape deck and sang along with it. She stood in front of the mirror, adding the gestures Ms. Kerry had taught her. She thought she looked pretty good.

She slipped out of her stage clothes and folded them up. Then she put her pajamas on and climbed into bed.

Chapter Ten

🞉

"ANGELA KING IS A KING-SIZE PIG"

This message was scrawled in red lipstick across the bathroom mirror in the girls' dressing room backstage.

"Who did this?" Angela demanded indignantly. She glanced around the room for evidence but didn't see any.

Her friends huddled around her. Angela forgot that she was mad at Sonya. All she felt was anger at the mirror-writer.

The girls trooped out of the bathroom, keeping their eyes open for somebody or something suspicious-looking. They saw Howard stoop to pick something up.

"Hey, look what I found," he exclaimed. He held out a pink makeup bag. "Does this belong to any of you?"

"No," the girls replied.

"Can I see it?" Angela asked. Howard handed the bag to her. She noted the tiny, smudged "Celia" handwritten in one corner. She peered inside the bag and pulled out a red lipstick with a flat, squashed tip.

"Look at that!" gasped Dawn.

Angela took the lipstick into the dressing room and compared its color with the color of the writing on the mirror. The girls crowded around her.

"I knew it was Celia all the time," declared Terri.

They trooped out of the dressing room for the second time.

"Can someone please tell me what's going on?" Howard asked.

Sonya explained.

"I'm telling the principal," said Howard. A few minutes later, he returned. "I told him," he announced. "The janitor will clean the mirror."

"Thanks, Howard," said Angela.

At that moment, the principal arrived. "Do you know who did this?" he asked the girls.

"We think it was Celia Forester," Angela told him.

The principal shook his head. "Not Celia. She's a wonderful student."

That's just the trouble, thought Angela. The teachers all thought Celia was too wonderful to do anything wrong. Of course, a couple of months ago, she'd cheated on a test and tried to blame Sonya. But the principal had probably forgotten about that by now. Nevertheless, Angela showed him the makeup bag and asked him to compare the red lipstick with the writing.

After the principal had left, Howard asked, "Do you really think Celia did it?"

"It had to be Celia Forester," said Terri. "Her name is on the bag. Anyway, who else would do something like that?"

"She *is* mean enough," Howard agreed. He looked at Angela. "Don't worry, Angela. You're not fat. You look really great."

Angela smiled. "Thanks," she said, feeling a million times better.

"You're welcome."

"We've got to think of a way to get back at Celia," said Terri.

"Dawn could poison her food," suggested Angela.

"No. Celia would get too much sympathy if she was dying," said Sonya.

"Let's put a curse on her," Howard offered. "I learned some good ones in Africa."

Angela looked at him with new interest. "Like what?"

"Well, some natives have spells for putting people to sleep, or giving them hiccups that won't stop," Howard explained.

"Can you imagine Celia trying to sing to Tony with the hiccups?" said Sonya, giggling.

"You know, we don't need a spell to wreck the play," Terri pointed out. "We could just get Celia to eat a big glob of peanut butter before she goes on stage."

"Nobody's that dumb, Terri," Sonya said. "Especially not Celia."

"The African natives sometimes say magic words or dance around," said Howard. "It works."

"I don't think that's very practical in this culture, though," said Terri.

"Yeah, maybe you're right," agreed Howard. He started to walk away.

"You won't say anything about a curse, will you, Howard?" Angela called after him.

He frowned. "Are you kidding? It was my idea, remember?"

The girls laughed. The janitor arrived with a bucket and rags. Angela watched the red words mix with suds and streak down the mirror. The janitor wiped the glass clean.

Angela went to class then, but all she thought about was how she was going to get her revenge.

"I hate the principal," said Terri while they were practicing at Dawn's house that afternoon. "He never believes you when you blame someone."

"If you blamed Sidney Offenpoff, he would believe you," said Sonya. Sidney Offenpoff was the worst kid in the sixth grade.

Angela couldn't stop thinking about revenge. "Hey, Dawn, didn't your brother buy some sneezing powder?" she asked suddenly.

Dawn's face lit up. "Hey, yeah. Maybe he'll let us use it."

"We could put it down Celia's dress," said Angela with a wicked gleam in her eyes. "She wouldn't be able to act. She'd be too busy sneezing."

"What a super idea!" exclaimed Terri.

The idea *was* super, thought Angela. She just had to figure out a way to get into the dressing room without anybody seeing her.

Chapter Eleven

The first dress rehearsal for *West Side Story* took place after school the next day. Shortly beforehand, Angela made a quick survey of the boys' and girls' dressing rooms and decided that she *could* sprinkle sneezing powder on Celia's white dress, but that she'd have to do it early in the morning when nobody was around.

Angela wore her red T-shirt to the rehearsal.

"Please change into a black shirt, Angela," Ms. Kerry said firmly. "That's the costume."

"I'm wearing this one, Ms. Kerry," Angela replied, just as firmly. "Anita's important and I want her to stand out."

"If I let you wear a different T-shirt, everyone will want to, and the cast will look like a rainbow," the teacher pointed out.

"But Celia gets to wear a dress," said Angela. "It's not fair."

"Celia's the central character," said Ms. Kerry in exasperation. "Besides, when you all wear black, it makes you work harder to distinguish your characters. Please do as you're told."

Angela gritted her teeth as she peeled off the red shirt and replaced it with a black one. Adults just didn't understand, she thought. But she was determined to have her own way. She would just save her red shirt for the real play.

Celia had frowned when she'd seen Angela's red shirt.

"Why did you want to wear red?" she asked her when the rehearsal was over.

Angela took a deep breath as though she were doing her exercises. "Because I'm important."

"Very funny," said Celia. "Nobody's going to notice *you*. Well, maybe they'll notice your size. Otherwise they'll be looking at me."

"Want to bet?" Angela said, planting her hands on her hips.

Celia just smiled.

The next morning, the day before the play, Angela and her friends arrived at school very early. Only the janitors and a few teachers were around.

They found the auditorium doors open. Mops were propped in buckets outside the door, which meant a janitor might be inside.

"This isn't a good time," whispered Angela. "Somebody's going to see us."

"Or hear us," added Dawn. "It's too quiet here."

"We're supposed to be outside. Come on," said Sonya, leading the way.

"We can come back at lunch," added Terri.

At lunchtime, Terri, Sonya, and Angela crept into the auditorium. It was empty. Angela took the bottle of sneezing powder from her purse and took it into the girls' dressing room. She found the closet where Celia's costume hung and sprinkled powder on the lacy front of the dress.

Terri came up behind her. "Let me have that a minute, Angela," she said, grabbing it out of her hand.

The powder spilled down Angela's sweat shirt. She felt a sneeze coming, and clamped her hand over her mouth.

"I don't think we should be doing this," Sonya spoke up nervously.

"Don't be a ba—" Terri started to say, but Sonya bumped into her then. The sneezing powder fell out of Terri's hand and hit the floor.

"Oh, no! I-I-I'm gonna sneeze, too!" cried Sonya, holding her nose.

Terri pulled the neck of her T-shirt up over her face to protect her from the powder. She knelt down to scoop it up. "We can't leave the evidence on the floor like this," she said in a scared, muffled voice.

"You're right," replied Angela. She looked around and

saw an uneven white trail that traveled from the closets halfway across the room to where Terri knelt.

"Come on," she said worriedly. "Terri, don't leave your fingerprints in that stuff."

"I won't," she said.

Dawn arrived then. She had left her duties as cafeteria monitor to risk helping her friends. Immediately she saw their trouble and scooped up some of the powder, but in her eagerness to help them, she tripped, dumping powder on the black costumes.

"Dawn, you idiot!" cried Angela. "Those are going to be worn by all the girls! Half the cast will be sneezing!" She pushed past Dawn and shook the powder off the top of the pile of T-shirts. It floated through the room like snow. Dawn plugged her nose.

Terri, Sonya, and Angela couldn't stand it anymore. The stuff was on everything, and up their noses. Every now and then a sneeze escaped from one of them. Angela had a sudden thought. What if she was Celia and found her dress messed up like this? She'd be really mad. It was a rotten thing to do to anyone.

Just then they heard footsteps. Angela's heart pounded.

"Quick! Put that stuff away. Let's get out of here!" she whispered loudly.

Terri pushed the loose powder into a paper bag and threw it in the garbage.

"Don't leave any evidence," Angela cried.

"I don't want to carry it," Terri replied.

Angela gave her a dirty look and fished the paper bag out of the garbage. Then she stuffed the empty sneezing powder bottle into her jeans pocket. She had so much powder on her fingers that she couldn't take a breath without wanting to sneeze. Her friends had squashed their hands against their mouths. When Angela looked at them, she wanted to laugh and sneeze at the same time.

The footsteps drew closer, then stopped. Angela froze. Her three friends tiptoed safely out into the hall, but Angela got turned around in the darkness and found herself wading through the folds of the stage curtains until she came to the stairs. She tested one to see if it squeaked. It didn't, so she walked down them very carefully.

"Hi," said a voice behind her.

Angela whirled around, screamed, and sneezed.

The person stood in the curtains and laughed. Angela thought the laugh sounded familiar but she couldn't tell whom it belonged to. It didn't matter. The only thought that crossed her mind was: I'm dead now.

Chapter Twelve

Howard emerged from the curtains, grinning.

Angela's heart flip-flopped. She was expecting the principal or Mrs. Kerry. "Wow, did you scare me!" she exclaimed. "What're you *doing* in here?" She sneezed again.

"I heard noises, so I came to see what was going on," Howard replied. "I thought you might be a robber."

"A robber? What would I rob?" asked Angela.

Howard shrugged. "I don't know. What *were* you doing?"

Angela's friends, who had been watching nervously from the hallway, tiptoed back into the auditorium. Sonya told Howard what was going on. "But you've got to promise not to tell anyone," she warned him.

"Promise," added Angela.

"I won't tell," Howard promised. "But I still think some

kind of spell would be better. With a spell, you don't leave fingerprints or other clues.''

Terri made a face. She was mad at Howard. ''You scared us!'' she told him indignantly. ''We thought you were a teacher.''

''We could get murdered for this,'' Angela murmured.

''Hey, where's the powder?'' asked Sonya worriedly.

Dawn giggled. ''I think it's all up our noses.''

''Do you have any left?'' asked Howard.

Angela presented him with the paper bag. ''Sneeze your heart out,'' she said. They all laughed.

Angela's friends walked back into the hall with Howard, but Angela stayed behind. She thought about the sneezing powder. Then she thought of what Ms. Kerry would think if she knew what Angela had done. And how Celia would be a big sneezing joke the next night, and everyone would laugh at her. Even though that seemed like fun, Angela knew she wasn't really playing fair. And she didn't want to ruin the play. If she was going to be in it, she wanted it to be good. On the other hand, Celia probably was the one who had written on the mirror, and she deserved something like this. She had been mean to Angela—but Angela didn't want to be meaner.

Suddenly, she turned and went back into the girls' dressing room. She yanked Celia's costume off the hanger and shook it out an open window. Then she did the same with the T-shirts.

Just as she was finishing, the worst thing in the world

happened. Angela heard a noise. She stiffened, a T-shirt in her hand. Ms. Kerry entered the dressing room.

"Angela, what are you doing in here?" she asked.

Angela felt her face grow hot. "Uh, I was looking for my T-shirt," she replied. "The red one."

"Oh, yes. Right." Ms. Kerry looked strangely at her.

Angela glanced at the box of T-shirts. Unfortunately, the red shirt was sitting on top. She couldn't take her eyes off the box and she couldn't meet Ms. Kerry's gaze.

But all Ms. Kerry said was, "Here it is. Right under your nose." She handed her the red shirt.

Angela laughed. "Thanks a lot, Ms. Kerry. I can't believe I didn't see it. It was in plain sight. Well, see you onstage."

Angela scooted out of the dressing room. Her heart felt as if it were somewhere around her ankles. She'd gotten caught trying to do a good deed!

She ran into Terri and Sonya in the hall. "What were you doing?" they asked. "We were ready to send out a search party."

"I changed my mind," Angela told them.

"About what?" Terri demanded.

Angela told them everything.

"Are you crazy? You want revenge, don't you?" Terri asked.

Angela sneezed. "Not like this."

"You're chickening out."

"I am *not* chickening out." Angela rubbed her nose to

keep from sneezing again. "I just thought it was a dumb idea."

"We *could* get in trouble," said Sonya.

"We almost *did* get in trouble," Angela pointed out. "Anyway, I was afraid the play would be really bad if we went through with the plan."

"Yeah, I see what you mean," Sonya agreed. "I'd sure be mad if I started sneezing in the middle of my lines. Angela, you did the right thing."

Angela looked at her in surprise. "Thanks!" she said. "I'm glad somebody thinks so."

Terri looked at them both in surprise. "Hey, that's the first nice thing you guys have said to each other. Are you through being mad at each other?"

Angela scowled at Sonya. "No, I'm still mad," she said.

"I'm still mad, too," Sonya muttered.

Terri whistled through her teeth. "You guys better stop it. You're going to be highly visible in this play. You don't want to embarrass our club by acting dumb, do you?"

Angela and Sonya shook their heads.

"I still think it would've been fun to see Celia trying to sneeze and sing at the same time, though," Terri added. "I hope you didn't get all the powder off her dress."

Angela giggled. "Stay tuned for the next episode."

On the night before the first performance, Angela decided to weigh herself. She hadn't checked her weight lately because she didn't want to think about it. The last time she had looked at the scale it had been depressing. But since she thought her new black jeans felt a little looser, she decided to check.

She stepped on the scale. She had lost weight! She lifted up her T-shirt and pulled the waistband out. Wow—she looked great! Her stomach had curves instead of bulges. She wasn't "King-size Angela" anymore. What Celia had written on the bathroom mirror wasn't true at all!

Angela strutted around her bedroom, delighted. Then she started to sing, "I feel pretty, oh, so pretty, I feel pretty and witty and bright—and I pity any girl who isn't me tonight."

"Angela! I'm home," her mother called. Mrs. King entered Angela's room and saw her dancing and singing in front of the mirror.

"You look lovely," she said. "Did you lose some more weight?"

"Yup," Angela replied proudly.

"Congratulations!" Her mother gave her a hug.

Angela noticed the "Before" picture on her mirror and got an idea. "Take a picture of me now, in this costume," she said.

"But I'll take pictures of you at the play, honey," Mrs. King replied.

"I might be fatter then," Angela said, handing her the Polaroid camera she'd been given on her last birthday.

Angela struck a pose like a model, so that her curves would show. Her mother snapped the picture.

Angela loved watching the slick black sheet lighten into a photo. Her shoulders, her hair, the posters on the wall all sharpened into focus. The blob of a face became eyes, a nose, and a mouth.

She studied the photo carefully. She looked a little fatter than in real life, she thought.

"The camera puts on pounds, Angie," Mrs. King said, reading her daughter's thoughts.

"That's why all those models are so skinny in real life," said Angela.

When her mom left the room, Angela made an "After" label for her new picture. One day soon she would go to the poster shop and have the picture blown up.

For the time being, she stuck the photo on her mirror next to the "Before" picture. Then she stood in the middle of the room, admiring her progress.

Chapter Thirteen

❀

"This is the most important day in the whole world, and I have to get a sore throat!" Angela grumbled.

It was the morning of the performance. Mrs. King shone a flashlight down Angela's throat. "It's definitely red," she said. "I'll make some tea with lemon and honey. Then gargle with salt water. That always helps."

Angela tried both and felt better. She started to sing.

"Don't strain your voice now, or you'll just croak," her mother warned.

"But I have to practice," Angela insisted.

The phone rang then. It was Terri.

"What's wrong with you?" she demanded. "You sound like a frog."

"Sore throat," said Angela. "Do you believe it?"

"You can't have a sore throat! This is High Visibility Day for us," exclaimed Terri.

"I'll be visible, I just might not be able to sing," said Angela.

"Listen, Sonya and Dawn and I will be over in about ten minutes. We have to have a meeting," said Terri abruptly. She hung up before Angela could protest.

Angela wondered why they had to have a meeting. What did they have to discuss? If they were the medical association, it could mean something.

A half hour later, the girls arrived.

Sonya stared at Angela's hair. "What are you doing in braids?" she cried. "You can't wear your hair in braids. You're supposed to look sophisticated."

"I'll look okay," said Angela. "I'm not going to wear them tonight." She pulled the rubber bands out of her hair. "How's that?"

"Better," said Sonya sullenly.

"Now the only problem is your voice," said Terri. *"West Side Story* starring Angela Frog."

"Just when I discover I've got a good voice, I lose it," Angela moaned. "It's not fair."

The girls watched a rerun of "Maureen Montclair" and then Angela's friends went home.

Angela worried all afternoon. She drank orange juice and tea, and gargled with salt water. She didn't talk at all so that she could save her voice.

But finally, she had to get ready. She put on the red T-shirt. Her mother gave her a red velvet ribbon to tie in her hair, and offered to help Angela with her makeup. "You want to stand out, Angie,'' she said, brushing color onto her cheeks.

When Angela saw what her mom had done, she said, ''Maybe I should just wear a big sign that says 'Look At Me.' ''

Mrs. King laughed.

When Angela arrived at Gladstone Elementary that evening, her mother dropped her off at the front door.

''I'll park the car,'' said Mrs. King. ''If I don't see you before the show starts, knock 'em dead, Angie.''

''Thanks, Mom,'' said Angela. As soon as her mother was out of sight, Angie rubbed some of the blush off her cheeks. She didn't want to look like Chuckles the Clown. Then she hurried inside to find her friends.

A bunch of people were standing around Celia Forester. Angela spotted Sonya.

''What's going on?'' she asked.

''Celia sneezed,'' said Sonya. ''She says she's got a cold.''

''Now we're even,'' said Angela, clearing her scratchy throat.

Sonya looked worried. ''Do you think Celia's really got a cold?''

''I'm not a doctor,'' said Angela crossly. Sonya kept making funny faces, making her eyebrows pop up and down.

Suddenly Angela realized what she meant. ''Oh, *that.*''

"The powder," murmured Sonya.

"Shhh!" Angela looked around to see if anyone had heard. "I don't know. Let's go get ready."

There was no way to know if Celia really had a cold or if she was sneezing because of some leftover sneezing powder. But Angela forgot about the cold when Ms. Kerry came backstage and issued a few instructions to the cast. When she finished talking, she focused on Angela, who stood out in her red T-shirt.

"I think you're right, Angela," Ms. Kerry said at last. "Anita is a feisty character. I believe we should make an exception where her costume is concerned. You may wear the red shirt."

"Thanks, Ms. Kerry! I think so, too," Angela replied, grinning.

Eddie Martin was also dressed differently, and that seemed right for the part of Tony. He wore a white cotton jacket over his black T-shirt and jeans. He smiled at Angela. She wondered what it would have been like to hug and kiss him. If she were playing Maria, she would have to do that.

Angela considered herself lucky that Anita and her boyfriend, Bernardo, made a lot of jokes and didn't hug. Hugging and kissing in front of the whole school would be totally embarrassing. It was the only bad part about playing Maria.

Ms. Kerry motioned for the students to be quiet. Angela could hear the auditorium filling up. She glanced nervously at Sonya, who glanced nervously back. Ms. Kerry made a short announcement about the play—and then it began.

Wanda Tetley, a girl with a squeaky voice, stepped onto the stage and read an introduction about the war between the two gangs, the Jets and the Sharks.

The music began to play. Every time Angela heard the music, she got goose bumps. Her eyes shone. She looked around and saw that the rest of the cast had grown quiet and was listening, too.

Angela smiled to herself. The boys were on first. They filed onto the dark stage.

With a clap of cymbals, the curtain went up. Applause and whistles filled the auditorium.

Howard started to sing, "When you're a Jet, you're a Jet all the way . . ."

Angela straightened her red T-shirt. This was it, her big moment.

Chapter Fourteen

⚘

"Scene Two—in the bridal shop. Maria and Anita are fixing up a dress for Maria to wear to a dance," Wanda announced.

Angela stood over Celia with a pair of scissors, pretending to snip the lace on her white dress. She would have liked to cut off Celia's nose.

Celia spoke her first line. "Why did my brother bring me here? I haven't had any excitement."

"He brought you to marry Chino," Angela, as Anita, said. Chino was Bernardo's friend, played by a boy named Jack Barry.

"When I look at Chino, nothing happens," grumbled Maria.

"What do you expect to happen?" asked Anita.

Giggles erupted in the audience.

"I don't know. Something," replied Maria dreamily.

Tommy Atwood entered. He played Bernardo, Anita's boyfriend and Maria's brother.

"Are you both ready to go?" he asked.

"Yes. It's important that I have a good time tonight," said Maria.

"Why?" asked Bernardo. Chino stood behind him, shuffling from one foot to the other.

"Because tonight is the beginning of my life as a young lady in America!" cried Maria. With that, Celia flounced off the stage, and colored streamers were thrown from the wings. One of them fell on Angela's head.

The audience clapped wildly.

Next came the dance scene in which Tony and Maria meet for the first time. Afterward, Tony sang the song, "Maria." Then Tony and Maria sang "Tonight" together, and Anita and Bernardo joined in from the other side of the stage.

Angela's and Eddie's voices soared above the others. The crowd clapped appreciatively. Celia shot Angela a poisonous glance.

Angela grinned.

Then Bernardo said, "Good night, Anita Josefina del Carmen, et cetera, et cetera, et cetera."

He exited.

Rosalia, played by Sonya, giggled. "That's a very pretty name, Et cetera."

The others groaned.

"We have many pretty names at home," Rosalia went on.

"If you like it so much at home, why don't you go back there? demanded Anita.

Then the girls launched into the song, "America."

Later, her sore throat forgotten, Angela sang a long solo of "Tonight." The audience applauded excitedly.

The fight began between Bernardo, Riff, and Tony. Eddie, playing Tony, picked up the rubber knife and the blade fell off. He looked down at the knife woefully.

"What do I do now?" he asked aloud.

The audience laughed. Angela thought, Oh, no, the play is a mess.

But Howard (Riff) replied, "Just pretend you've got a real knife, Eddie."

So Eddie took the knife shaft and pretended to stab Bernardo. Both Bernardo and Riff fell to the floor, dead.

The audience was laughing wildly. It isn't supposed to be funny, thought Angela.

A scene followed that featured all the girls. Sonya had a big part, singing in Rosalia's screechy voice. Angela glanced at her and smiled. She smiled back. Maybe they were through being mad with each other. Certainly, Angela didn't have to worry about Sonya stealing any attention from her. The audience loved Angela. Angela decided she could forgive Sonya for laughing at Celia's comments. She knew Sonya hadn't meant to hurt her feelings.

The play went on. The other gang members found out

about the killings. Chino went to tell Maria, who started sobbing loudly.

Celia really is a good actress, Angela thought, as Celia looked at the audience with tear-filled eyes.

Tony approached Maria, wanting to talk to her.

"Killer!" she yelled at him, and then stomped on his foot.

Eddie drew away. "Ouch!"

The audience laughed.

"Move your big feet," said Celia in annoyance.

"Sorry. Oh, Maria, I want you to forgive me," said Tony in a rush. "So I can go to the police."

"No, stay with me," pleaded Maria. She yanked on Tony's sleeve. Then they started to sing as the gang members ran between them.

The scene changed to a drugstore where Tony and Maria were supposed to meet so they could run away together. Anita was there, waiting with Maria.

Anita yelled, "A boy like Tony is no good. What do you want with him?" (Angela loved this part. It gave her a chance to do some serious acting.)

"Anita, I love him," said Maria in a weepy voice.

Then Tony saw Maria and they ran to each other. A shot was fired from a cap gun and Tony fell into her arms.

Angela, standing close to them, heard what Celia whispered at that touching moment.

"Eddie, you're too heavy. Will you stop hanging on me!"

Eddie ignored her. "Maria!" he cried.

Maria pushed him off, then knelt down to cradle his head in her arms. She leaned down and kissed the top of his head. "I love you, Tony," she said.

The students giggled hysterically, but when the curtain fell, the crowd went wild.

The cast walked back on stage to take their bows. Somebody handed a bouquet of red roses to Celia. Angela stood right next to her and could feel the roses brush against her bare skin.

"Yeah, Anita!" shouted Terri and Dawn from the first row of seats. "Yeah, Rosalia!"

Then Dawn carried a bunch of handpicked dandelions and daisies onto the stage and gave some to both Angela and Sonya. "I picked them myself," she said proudly.

"Thanks, Dawn," Angela said. The flowers looked sort of tacky next to Celia's bouquet, but neither Sonya nor Angela cared.

Afterward, Ms. Kerry took Angela aside. "You sang beautifully," she told her. "Do you think you could convince your mother to sign you up for singing lessons?"

Angela shrugged. "I never thought about it, but I guess so."

"What about me, Ms. Kerry?" demanded Celia, who was standing nearby.

"You sang nicely, too, Celia," she said. "You did very well. And those are lovely roses."

Ms. Kerry turned back to Angela. "Come see me on Monday morning. We can have a chat then."

Celia scowled. She opened her mouth to say something, but just then Angela's mom appeared and enveloped Angela in a hug.

"Angie, congratulations!" she cried. "You were wonderful! What a great performance. Today Gladstone, tomorrow Broadway!"

Angela untangled herself from her mother. "Thanks, Mom." She could feel herself turning red, but she was so happy, it didn't matter.

"Angie, we must celebrate," her mother said enthusiastically. "There's a fabulous little restaurant that I've been just *dying* to try."

Angela groaned. Her friends laughed. Some things never changed.

About the Author

SUSAN SMITH was born in Great Britain and has lived most of her life in California. She began writing when she was thirteen years old and has authored a number of successful teenage novels, including the *Samantha Slade* series published by Archway Paperbacks. Currently, she lives in Brooklyn with her two children. Both children have provided her with many ideas and observations that she has included in her books. In addition to writing, Ms. Smith enjoys travel, horseback riding, skiing, and swimming.

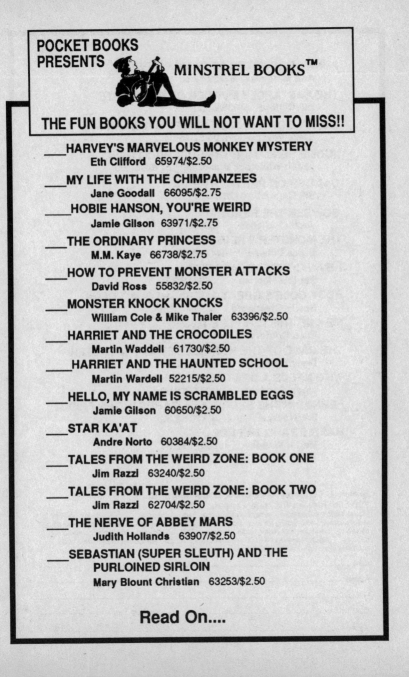

___**PUNKY BREWSTER AT CAMP CHIPMUNK**
    Ann Matthews 62729/$2.50

___**THE DASTARDLY MURDER OF DIRTY PETE**
    Eth Clifford 55835/$2.50

___**ME, MY GOAT, AND MY SISTER'S WEDDING**
    Stella Pevsner 66206/$2.75

___**JUDGE BENJAMIN: THE SUPERDOG RESCUE**
    Judith Whitelock McInerney 54202/$2.50

___**DANGER ON PANTHER PEAK**
    Bill Marshall 61282/$2.50

___**BOWSER THE BEAUTIFUL**
    Judith Hollands   63906/$2.50

___**THE MONSTER'S RING**
    Bruce Colville   64441/$2.50

___**KEVIN CORBETT EATS FLIES**
    Patricia Hermes 66881/$2.75

___**ROSY COLE'S GREAT AMERICAN GUILT CLUB**
    Sheila Greenwald   63794/$2.50

___**ME AND THE TERRIBLE TWO**
    Ellen Conford   63666/$2.50

___**THE CASE OF THE HORRIBLE SWAMP MONSTER**
    Drew Stevenson 62693/$2.50

___**WHO NEEDS A BRATTY BROTHER?**
    Linda Gondosh   62777/$2.50

___**FERRET IN THE BEDROOM, LIZARDS IN THE FRIDGE**
    Bill Wallace   61730/$2.50

___**HARRIET AND THE ROBOT**
    Martin Waddell   66021/$2.50

Simon & Schuster Mail Order Department MMM
200 Old Tappan Rd., Old Tappan, N.J. 07675
Please send me the books I have checked above. I am enclosing $_____ (please add 75¢ to
cover postage and handling for each order. N.Y.S. and N.Y.C. residents please add appro-priate
sales tax). Send check or money order--no cash or C.O.D.'s please. Allow up to six weeks for
delivery. For purchases over $10.00 you may use VISA: card number, expiration date and
customer signature must be included.

Name _____

Address _____

City _____ State/Zip _____

VISA Card No. _____ Exp. Date _____

Signature _____184-02